Polar Bear Cub

by Jacqueline Moody-Luther
Illustrated by Cathy Trachok

To Jackson Race, my curly-headed cub. I live for your bear hugs. — J.L.

Published by Soundprints Division of Trudy Corporation, Norwalk, Connecticut

Book design: Marcin Pilchowski
Editor: Ben Nussbaum
Production Editor: Brian E. Giblin

First Edition 2006
10 9 8 7 6 5 4 3 2
Printed in China

Acknowledgments:
Our very special thanks to Dr. Don E. Wilson of the Department of Systematic Biology at the Smithsonian Institution's National Museum of Natural History for his curatorial review.
Soundprints would also like to thank Ellen Nanney and Katie Mann at the Smithsonian Institution's Office of Product Development and Licensing for their help in the creation of this book.

Library of Congress Cataloging-in-Publication Data is on file with the publisher and the Library of Congress.

Polar Bear Cub

by Jacqueline Moody-Luther

Illustrated by Cathy Trachok

A note to the reader:
Throughout this story you will see words in **bold letters**. There is more information about these words in the glossary. The glossary is in the back of the book.

A winter storm blows. It is very cold outside. Inside a **den**, two polar bear cubs are born. They press against their mother's fur to stay warm.

The cubs grow
without ever
leaving the den.
The family will
stay in the den
all winter.

Soon spring is here.

Time to go outside!

Cub walks out into

the sunshine for

the first time.

Cub's mother waits by a hole in the ice to catch a **seal**. Cub and her brother play in the snow.

Cub sees a fox.
Cub's mother
chases the
fox away.

Each day is warmer. The ice is breaking up into pieces. Cub and her family will **travel** to land.

Cub's mother jumps over the water to another piece of ice. Cub must follow her! Cub leaps into the air.

She lands near
her mother! Her
brother jumps too.

Now the family
must swim to land.
It is far away. But
Cub and her brother
are good swimmers.

Cub swims in the cold water. Her **blubber** keeps her warm.

After a long swim, Cub arrives on land. Her family will stay here for the summer. Now it's time for a nap!

Glossary

Blubber: A thick layer of fat that helps keep some animals warm.

Den: A small, comfortable area where animals live.

Seal: A fast-swimming animal with stiff whiskers and flippers.

Travel: To move around from one place to another.

About Polar Bears

Polar bears live in the frigid Arctic. They cannot be found farther south than James Bay, Canada. Few polar bears ever travel to the northern Arctic because it is hard for them to find seals, which are their main source of food.

Polar bears are excellent swimmers and live near water. They prefer to live on sea ice that has leads, which are cracks through the ice that make it easy to hunt seals.

Polar bears can appear white, yellow, or even brown, depending on the season. Their bodies are longer and they have more slender necks than most bears. Polar bears are the largest land carnivores, or meat eaters, and they have 42 teeth. When not hunting, polar bears sleep or rest.

Other animals that live near polar bears:

Arctic foxes   Walruses

Reindeer   Whales

Seals

Polar bears can appear white, yellow, or even brown, depending on the season. Their bodies are longer and they have more slender necks than most bears. Polar bears are the largest land carnivores, or meat eaters, and they have 42 teeth. When not hunting, polar bears sleep or rest.

Other animals that live near polar bears:

Arctic foxes   Walruses

Reindeer   Whales

Seals